Abraham's
Battle

Abraham's Battle

A Novel of Gettysburg

Sara

Harrell

Banks

SCHOLASTIC INC.

New York Toronto London Auckland Sydney
Mexico City New Delhi Hong Kong

Grateful acknowledgement is made to Harriet Stovall Kelley for permission to excerpt her poem, "Foxhill Housewarming," which appears in *Look Back, Beholden,* copyright 1998, and reprinted by permission of Hask.

ISBN 0-439-28302-7

12 11 10   7 8 9 10/0

Printed in the U.S.A.   40

First Scholastic printing, February 2001

Book design by Nina Barnett
The text of this book is set in Sabon.

Thank God there's more than all we know,
For greater oaks than we can grow,
For lamplight, when the sun has gone,
And for a wood to wonder on.

—Harriet Stovall Kelley

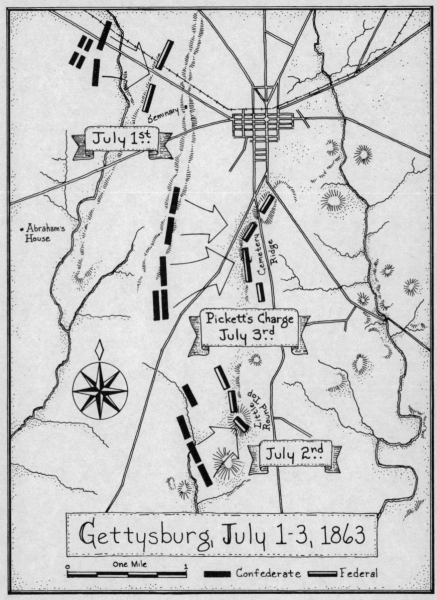

July 1st.

Seminary

Abraham's House

Pickett's Charge July 3rd.

Cemetery Ridge

Little Round Top

July 2nd.

Gettysburg, July 1-3, 1863

0 One Mile 1 ████ Confederate ══════ Federal

Map by Rick Britton

Prologue

November 18, 1863—Gettysburg, Pennsylvania

The train whistle, low and mournful, wound its way over fields lying fallow in the autumn dusk. It drifted among the bare branches of a cherry tree where an owl stared with great golden eyes.

Whooo? became part of the sound that curved around the eaves of the barn, causing Charity to prick up her soft mule ears. Finally, the fading notes crept through the shuttered windows of a cottage where an old man sat sewing in the lamplight. He raised his head, listening intently. And when the whistle died, he looked over at the clock in the corner.

Tick-tock . . . tick-tock . . . tick-tock . . . the seconds dropped smooth as polished stones on the quiet air.

"They gon' be pullin' into the station any minute

now," he said to Enoch, the gray-striped cat that lay curled up in a basket near the hearth. Enoch gazed over at Abraham with amber eyes, his cat's face crumpled with sleep. He yawned, showing tiny, sharp teeth, then put his head back down on his paws.

"Well," said Abraham, "maybe you can sleep, but I sure can't. Mr. Abraham Lincoln, the president of the United States himself, is coming right here to Gettysburg to make a speech." He nodded his head in the cat's direction. "And as for myself, old Abraham Small, ex-slave, freeman now, I am making plans to be there."

He placed a patch on his coat where it had worn thin, turning the edges under with briar stitching. His hands seemed too big and rough to sew a fine seam, but it was something his mama had taught him. His mama, Rebecca, had been a slave called Becky. He'd watched her, time and again, as she worked by firelight, sewing the seams of dresses she'd never wear and never own. She sewed for the white gentry who owned the cotton fields, the plantation, the horses, mules, and cattle, and the slaves.

"Abraham," she'd say after supper. "Fetch me my basket, please." And he'd bring the sewing basket that held her thimble, darning egg, thread, and needles. Woven of pine needles and grasses, it smelled sweet. And while he hated that she had to work so hard, he loved sitting by her side as she sewed. After she'd made a dress for the mistress, Becky would be allowed to keep the scraps. She'd cut out neat squares and patterns for patchwork quilts and aprons. One evening, as she was making church dollies, she'd turned to Abraham.

"Did you think to save me some bolls?" she asked.

"Yes'm," he'd replied, taking the cotton bolls that he'd brought inside from the day's pickings from his overall pockets. She'd put one in the center of a neatly hemmed square of cloth, tied a ribbon around it to form a head, then fluffed it out to make a dolly. Little girls took them to church, and if a dolly fell on the floor, it didn't disturb anyone.

His sweet mama was in heaven now, and he had his freedom. And Mr. Lincoln had declared that there wasn't going to be any more slavery; not anymore and not ever again. He bit off the thread and smoothed the patch with a rough hand.

"Bad as I want to hear the speechifying, I don't believe it's fittin' to go see the president in this raggedy old coat. But it's all I've got." He put his mama's sewing basket away and looked at the clock again. Time to feed Charity and let her know what's going on.

At the doorway he threw a tattered shawl over his shoulders and stepped out into the cool night that held the lingering fragrance of woodsmoke. The evening star hung low over the barn. He started to make a wish; for a new coat and a new hat. Then he stopped. *Mr. Lincoln will see my heart tomorrow,* he thought, *not my old coat and bare head.*

The barn was warm with the breath of animals and smelled of hay. Charity watched him, her eyes dark and liquid in the lamplight.

Abraham gave Charity fresh oats and carrots. As he watched her eat, he began talking. He always talked to her. It was just his way of thinking a thing through, and no one could deny she was a good listener. "The president's coming here tomorrow for the dedication of the National Cemetery. And we're gon' see him. We've been invited to ride in the parade on account of what we did during the battle in July." Taking a brush from the side of the stall, he began grooming the mule's coat until it gleamed like dark velvet.

"You know they call this the 'Civil War'? Ain't nothin' civil about it, far's I can tell. Anyway, you recall how our part in it all started? You and me and Ladysmith were out in the garden when Lamar stopped by to talk. It was the last of June, just before the battle."

Chapter 1

The last day of June 1863

Charity waited for Abraham in the warm sweetness of the barn. At the sound of his footsteps, she pricked up her long ears. The door opened and morning light spilled in, hazing her coat with gold. Pigeons roosting in the rafters rose in a spiral toward the sun-filled roof. Abraham cocked his head at the flutter of wings; he was hearing rustlings that seemed to come from both inside and outside the barn.

Up the hill Mrs. Lightly stood at the kitchen window of the white house. Crisp gingham curtains framed cherry trees laden with fruit. She looked past the trees to where the roof of the barn was barely visible. "I don't see anybody," she said to Ladysmith, who was eating breakfast. "I know they're out there, but I just don't know where."

Ladysmith looked up from where she was making roads and valleys in her bowl of porridge. "We probably won't even see any soldiers, Mother," she said soothingly, her pale hair lit by the early morning sun. Using the bowl of her spoon, Ladysmith made a lake in her porridge and waited while it filled with milk. She hated the stuff, and at ten years old, felt she was too old to have to eat it. Porridge was for babies. Besides, if she so much as *touched* a lump, it made her feel sick. But she didn't complain. She didn't want to upset her mother any more than she already was, and have her change her mind about letting her go to the orchard with Abraham and Charity.

But Mrs. Lightly *was* fretting, running from one window to the next, looking for soldiers behind every tree. Ladysmith knew she was worried about the upcoming battle, which was bound to take place near their town of Gettysburg. Only nobody knew exactly where or when it would happen.

The delicious smell of cherry tarts baking filled the kitchen, distracting Mrs. Lightly from her vigil at the window. Removing the hot pastries from the big woodstove, she placed them gingerly into a basket. "I used our last bit of sugar for these," she said to Ladysmith. "Take them for your picnic. Heaven knows when we'll get more."

Ladysmith's boots made deep prints in the dew-laden grass as she hurried across the backyard, past the washhouse, the smokehouse, and down the hill to the paddock. At the gate she tried the latch, but it was rusty and refused to open. *Abraham'll be gone before I get there,* she fretted, giving the gate a swift kick. Then, putting the basket down, she climbed the fence, tumbling over in a froth of petticoats. By the time she sorted herself out again, Abraham was leading Charity from the barn.

"It's not fair," she said as he helped her onto the mule's back. "Girls ought to be allowed to wear trousers. Then I could ride properly, instead of sidesaddle. And I could climb fences better!"

"I hadn't noticed it slowed you down any," said Abraham mildly, in a voice that came from deep in his chest. The three of them ambled slowly down the hill from the Lightlys' house. One hundred years earlier, Ladysmith's great-grandfather had built this house on a gentle rise in a grove of trees way out in the woods. But over time the town had grown and was now only a few miles east. Still, the fine old trees protected the house from harsh winds in winter and offered shade in the long summers.

Golden sunflowers turned heavy heads toward the sun. Crows flew inky black against the bright blue sky. Abraham was on his hands and knees, picking the crookneck squash nearly hidden under broad leaves. When his basket was full, he stood up shakily, his old knees popping. *Wish I could just plant crops I could stand up to pick,* he mused. *Okra would be good.* He couldn't get the seeds, though. Seemed like folks up north didn't plant okra. Could be that it wouldn't grow so far up as Pennsylvania. He wasn't sure. But his stand of corn was as fine as any he'd grown at home, the leaves shiny green, the ears tassling like spun silk. As he walked the rows that were shoulder high, he was grateful to the Lord for such a good crop.

"Abraham!" called Ladysmith, her high voice as fluting as a little bird's. "Somebody's coming!"

From the end of the corn row, Abraham looked down the slope toward the snake-rail fence that separated the Lightlys' property from the road. Ladysmith was perched on Charity's back, watching as a lone soldier came down the dusty road. It was a Johnny Reb in a faded uniform, his feet bare as a yard dog's.

Pulling his hat down so that the brim shaded his eyes, Abraham started down the slope. "Ladysmith," he said when he neared the fence, "you and Charity ride on over to that patch of Yankee clover till I find out what this man wants." He felt uneasy, wary of this Confederate just showing up.

Ladysmith hesitated. It seemed like grown-ups were always sending her off while they "talked." It was as silly as Abraham calling red clover "Yankee" just because where he came from, clover was white.

"Go on, now," Abraham said. "Your mama didn't leave you in my care to have somethin' happen to you."

Clucking softly to the mule, Ladysmith rode off. A moment later, while Charity cropped the tender flowers, she pretended to search for a four-leaf clover for good luck, but kept an eye on the two men.

Although this was the third summer of the Civil War, the people in Gettysburg hadn't been much affected. The battles had been fought in other places. Up to now, Abraham hadn't had much truck with soldiers. Oh, he'd seen them off in the distance across the valley, but he sure hadn't had anything to do with a Confederate. But now the war was drawing nearer. Earlier in the month,

General Robert E. Lee, the commander of the Army of Northern Virginia, had moved his troops north. And the Army of the Potomac, under General George G. Meade, was moving from Maryland in the South toward Lee's army. These armies—the Confederate and Union forces—would meet and fight at Gettysburg.

The little town of twenty-four hundred citizens was situated like the center of a web, with nine roads leading into it. Those roads would soon be filled with long lines of soldiers in blue and gray, and the dust-spattering hoofs of cavalry. But that wouldn't happen for a day yet.

Soft dust puffed and settled on the soldier's feet when he stopped and looked over at Abraham. The two reached the fence at about the same time, Abraham on one side, the soldier on the other. For a moment neither spoke. Then the soldier nodded politely. "Mornin'," he said. "How y'all?"

Abraham was startled by the first southern accent he'd heard since arriving up North four years earlier. The softness of it fell on his ears like rain on a parched land. He thought it was a Georgia accent, but not of the low country where he came from; this was denser, with a rough twang. He nodded, but didn't say anything. After all, this boy was the enemy. He waited, the silence stretched out between them like a thin cord.

The soldier looked over to where Charity was cropping sweet clover.

"A good molly mule's a purty thang," he said. "And you don't see a dark brown coat that often. Least, not in my part of the country. She change color as she got older?"

"Her foal coat was pretty much that dark," said Abraham, speaking for the first time, pleased in spite of himself that Charity's fine qualities were appreciated. As if she knew they were talking about her, Charity stretched her neck and turned sideways. Her tail was braided and her forelock shaved to a neat fringe.

"And where might your part of the country be?" Abraham asked.

"North Georgia," was the reply. "Up around Rabun Gap."

Ladysmith couldn't stand being left out of the conversation, so she climbed down off Charity's back, then walked quietly over to the fence. She'd never seen a rebel soldier up close before and didn't know what to expect. She looked at the tall, lanky soldier in the faded uniform as he stood squinting into the sun, his canvas haversack over one shoulder. Then, glancing down at his bare feet, she asked, "What happened to your shoes?"

"Done walked 'em off," he said. "I come up all the way from the South to the North."

"Why, you poor thing," said Ladysmith. "Does it hurt to march?"

"My feet are tougher'n lightard knots," he replied, looking out toward the distant hills. He appeared to be thinking hard on something. Finally, he turned and stuck his hand over the fence to Abraham.

"Name's Cooper," he said. "Private Lamar Cooper. Don't believe I caught your name."

Abraham reflected that this was only the second time in his life that a white man had ever thought to shake his hand. He hesitated for a moment. But then, removing his hat, he held out his own hand. "Abraham Small. Freeman."

"Pleased," said Lamar, drawing a long breath. "You from the South too. How come you to be up here?"

Nodding his head toward Ladysmith, Abraham replied, "I work for her daddy. He's in the army too, the *Union* army," he said pointedly. He spoke more carefully now, not sure how much to say to this soldier boy. When all was said and done, he was fightin' for the other side; the *wrong* side. Still, Abraham couldn't see how the boy could do any harm to him here.

"Before he joined the army, Mr. Lightly was a conductor for the Underground Railroad," Abraham went on. "It was him helped me get here from down near Savannah." *It was Mr. Lightly who first shook my hand.*

"So you come up on the train?" Lamar asked, clearly confused.

Abraham looked at him, at his blue eyes that were eager to please. "How old are you?" he asked.

"Sixteen last April."

"The Underground ain't a railroad," Abraham explained, leaning on the fence. "It was a way for slaves to escape. It ain't there no more, the route closed down when the war started." He remembered a church, the First African Baptist in Savannah. It was the first stop on his railroad journey. They'd hidden him in a tiny space, dark, not big enough to sit up straight in, under the altar. They helped him at great risk since they too were colored. But Abraham saw no need to give Lamar too many details.

Lamar looked at Abraham keenly, as if trying to read something in his face. "If you'll pardon me for sayin' so, you're the first slave I ever met."

"*Ex*-slave," Abraham corrected him. And when Lamar nodded in acknowledgment, Abraham continued. "Folks helped us till we reached a safe place. Mine turned out to be here, working for the Lightlys. Now I gets paid for my work. I got my own house and I takes care of their place and the animals."

"He takes care of me, too," said Ladysmith.

"She's in my charge," Abraham said. Then, curious as to why Lamar was off by himself, he inquired, "You lost? Or scoutin'? 'Cause if you're scoutin' for food, I can tell you right now most of what's growing or has legs has been carted off. Rebs have shucked this land like an ear of corn. The cherry orchards are bare and there ain't a pig to be found. Soldiers already took everything but the squeal."

He glanced back at his own garden. So far, nobody'd bothered it, but he knew it was not because of any tenderness of heart on either side. It was just that it was small and out of the way and nobody'd noticed it.

"I ain't scoutin' for food," said Lamar. "My orders are not to take anything we don't actually need. I'm with Lieutenant General James Longstreet," he added proudly, as if by giving his commander's name, it explained something. And to him it did; it implied a decency even in war.

"We're running kind of short of things now, 'specially medicines. The ambulance corps is in a bad bind. So Doc Fairlie, one of the doctors in our regiment, asked me to scout for yarbs and such. He knows how to make medicines from stuff like blackberry, sweet gum, Solomon's seal for wounds . . ."

Abraham nodded. "My mama knew 'bout that kind of healin'."

"And pennyroyal. We need lots of that," said Lamar. "You know where that grows around here?"

"Y'all troubled by fleas," Abraham stated flatly.

"That's a pure fact," Lamar admitted. "*And* lice. We got so many that I caught some with C. S., that stands for Confederate States," he explained, "inscribed on their backs. In fact we got a poem:

Now I lay me down to sleep,
While gray-backs o'er my body creep;
If I should die before I wake,
I pray the Lord their jaws to break."

Abraham's laughter rang out, and when Lamar joined in, there was an easing between them, the way the air calms after a storm.

"If my daddy gets them, he's gonna' be *hopping* mad!" Ladysmith announced, which made them laugh even harder.

After thinking about it for a little while, Abraham asked Ladysmith, who knew every inch of the place, to lead the way to where purple-flowered pennyroyal dusted the slopes of the sunny meadow. *After all,* he thought, *herbs, or "yarbs" as Lamar calls them, are for healin'. Cain't be any harm in that. It ain't like I'm helping him make bullets. We're just easin' somebody's misery.*

Chapter 2

Abraham, Ladysmith, and Lamar picked handfuls of pennyroyal until they'd filled a croker sack. Then they walked back across the meadow where summer butterflies danced over the white blooms of Queen Anne's lace. When they reached the orchard, Lamar shifted his sack from one shoulder to the other. "Mind if I set a spell?" he asked. "I walked a tolerable long way today."

"Rest yourself," said Abraham, motioning toward an old tree that offered shade.

"So what was it you did, back in Georgia?" Lamar asked as they made themselves comfortable. Charity rolled on her back in the sunshine.

"What you think?" said Abraham, raising his eyebrows almost to his forehead. "I owned a plantation?"

Then he continued. "I told you, I was a slave. At first I worked as a field hand. Then I worked in the stables. When the mistress saw I was good with animals, she let me drive her carriage, made me a coachman. Had me a fine suit to wear too, but it didn't actually belong to me. I'd take the ladies to their parties and to town to shop. Pretty soon, the master was lending me out to other plantation owners. I drove all over that place. That's how come I was able to learn to read. Had to do it in secret, though. Man owned me, wouldn't allow it." He shook his head as if clearing it of bad memories. "Next place over was a fella taught me. He was a slave too, but his owners let him learn so's he could help count at the cotton exchange in Savannah. They set great store by him."

"Tell you the truth, I never pondered much on slavery," said Lamar.

Never pondered? Never thought 'bout a human being treated like property by another human being? For a moment Abraham couldn't speak for the sudden anger that welled up inside him. "I'm gon' tell you about a thing you *can* ponder on," he said fiercely, once again aware that this boy was the enemy, even if he was young and didn't know 'bout much. "It's a bad thing. You wish to hear of it?"

Lamar nodded, surprised by Abraham's sudden fierceness. He leaned his head against the trunk of the tree. "Go right ahead," he said.

"It was a long time ago," said Abraham. "I come back from drivin' the mistress and her friends to Savannah to shop. We was ridin' down the alley of live oaks leading up to the big house when I heard somebody call me out by my name. I seen a wagon up under a tree holdin' my wife and two more. My heart 'bout stopped, but I had to go on and take the ladies to the front door. When I come back I hear Jiji, my wife, cryin', and I started over to the wagon to fetch her. But Mr. Hamm, the overseer for the place, warned me off. 'You, Abraham!' he yelled. 'Keep away from the wagon!' Then he tole me how the three of 'em been sold."

"Lordamercy," said Lamar softly.

"I axed him, jest let me talk to her. But he said for me not to come no closer than ten feet to the wagon. Jiji was cryin' so hard it broke my heart. I begged him again, please let me talk to her. 'You can tell her good-bye is all,' he said. Then they was gone. I never was able to learn where she went, I never saw her again. They said in the cabins that she'd been sold at the slave market in Charleston, but I don't know."

"Why'd they sell her?" Lamar asked, fanning his face with his cap.

Abraham shrugged. "They didn't need no reason. Money maybe. She was a strong woman and a good worker. And I loved her," he added softly.

Ladysmith wiped her eyes on her sleeve. Even though she knew about Abraham's wife, hearing the story made her sorrowful all over again.

"That was the day I made up my mind to get away," Abraham continued. "I wanted to run, but if I'd been caught, they'd have whupped me so bad I'd wouldn't have had the strength to try again. So I started working every day I could, getting off the place every chance I got. My heart hurt so bad I felt like I was gonna die. But I kept on keepin' on. I pondered and connived from that day. Least, I was better off than most bein' a driver and able to get off the place. And I heard things. So when help was offered, I took it. Someone helped fix me up with the Underground and I *left* that place. I left it before emancipation! Before Mr. Lincoln freed the slaves!"

But even as he was explaining this to Lamar, something caught in Abraham's mind like cloth catching on a thorn. A tiny prick of a thing, like a warning, or a new idea. He pushed it back, unwilling to think it through.

He'd had that same feeling in his head, in his mind, before. It happened on the day they took Jiji away. Something terrible died in him and something else grew, something strong and fierce and angry.

Lamar was twisting his cap around and around in his hands.

"I surely didn't intend to hurt your feelin's when I asked about what you did back home," he said, his pale eyes anxious. "Fact is, I never even knew a colored man before. And I sure didn't know no slaves. What I mean is, there wasn't any slaves where I come from in the mountains. Wasn't no plantations neither. Just farmers making a hard scrabble livin'."

"You was poor?" asked Abraham. He hadn't known many poor whites.

"Too poor to paint, too proud to whitewash," Lamar replied. "I got me a mule, though," he said. "He's blind. 'Cain't do much except grind corn for meal."

"What's his name?" Ladysmith asked, intrigued by the thought of a blind mule.

"Jes' Mule," Lamar replied.

"Jesmule?" she asked, thinking what a funny name that was.

"No," he said. "Jes' . . . 'Mule.'" He smiled when she

giggled and continued. "When this war started it seemed like a good way to have a little fun. I joined up when I was fourteen. And I wasn't the youngest in my outfit. One boy was thirteen, but he was big for his age. I venture to say that most of the ones not officers is around the age of eighteen. At first, we all figgered the whole thing'd be over in no time a'tall. Why, ever'body knew a Johnny could whup seven Yankees anytime." He glanced over at Ladysmith who had filled her lap with flowers and was weaving daisy chains. "No insult intended, little lady," he said.

"But I learnt quick that fightin' wasn't no fun. I never seen men die before. Least, not in battle. My folks was dead, but they died in an accident on the mountain. So when I went off to fight, I didn't have nobody but my sister. I saw battle at Manassas. Even though they say we won, that fight was a turrible thang. When I seen wounded layin' on the ground thick as a drove of hogs, I had to wonder why."

Ladysmith looked up from her flowers. "Oh, Lamar," she said mournfully. "You've got no mama and no papa and no shoes. You should just stay here with us."

"Which side you on?" Abraham chided her gently.

"Ours!" she declared. "But he's a poor orphan."

Abraham shook his head and motioned for Lamar to continue.

"Some say they'd go back to the Union 'stead of all this killin'," the boy went on. "And I know that many would say that's not right. But I want them to come and see and feel what I have and they would feel the same. Fact is, after a while, I wasn't sure jest why I was fightin'." He said this with great relief, as though glad to have it off his chest.

"What it amounts to in my eyes is we got a bunch of poor boys fightin' a rich man's war. And as far as secession goes, why, we don't have but one man in the entire company's a secesh."

"Tell me again what that word means," Ladysmith interrupted.

"Somebody wants to leave the Union, the United States of America," replied Lamar. " 'Cause they hate Yankees or they're scairt that President Lincoln's gon' take their rights away from 'em. Most folks left the Union because they figgered they had a right to own slaves in their own states. Didn't want no President Lincoln tellin' them what they could or couldn't do. 'Course, I figure that means if you *had* slaves." He looked over at Abraham. "I didn't know a thang about that," he said apologetically. "But I did believe that states' rights was only fair. Folks in the South figgered that their rights wouldn't be worth a toot under President Lincoln, so that's why they seceded. All the newspapers said so."

"This war's 'bout slavery," said Abraham. "Pure and simple. Don't nobody have the right to own another human being. Nobody. And that's a truth I'd lay down and die for." Again, that tiny thorn in his head pricked sharply. "That might not be why some are fightin', but that's what this war's about." Then he said, "So explain to me again why you fightin' against the Union?"

"I ain't exactly fightin' *against* it," Lamar said, looking offended. "It's more like I'm fightin' *for* the South. I cain't hep' what some fool politician does, getting everybody all het up about seceding from the Union and then we got to go along with it. But we cain't have the federal gov'mint tellin' us what to do and all. When Georgia seceded, I had to go along with it, didn't I? What I mean is, Georgia's my home."

Abraham picked a stalk of sourweed and chewed it slowly. "I reckon this is my home now, but it wasn't easy settlin' in." He thought back to his first days in Gettysburg. "Early on, a woman shot at me," he said. "All's I was after was directions to Mr. Matthew Lightly's house. But she didn't let me finish, just hauled off and shot at me. Missed me, though."

"That was old lady Bellinder," piped up Ladysmith, pointing across the fields. "That's her farm over there. She's just hateful."

"Why'd she do that?" Lamar asked.

"I axed Mr. Lightly about it," Abraham replied, "and he said 'cause she didn't know me. And 'cause I'm colored. I used to think that things was jest bad for us down South. And they were! But there's folks everywhere don't like anybody different from them, I discovered."

"That don't give her the right to shoot at you," said Lamar. "Folks is jes' plain peculiar when you think on it. I figgered when I got in the army, I'd meet all kinds. I never even been away from home till I joined the army. Never even got a letter till then. Shucks, never even *wrote* one before that." He looked out at the wooded hills dotted with barns and farmhouses. "Back home, barns are gray instead of red," he said wistfully. "It's sure different up here. I mean, ever'thang's different. I have to tell you, first time I heard a bunch of Yankees talkin', I thought they sounded like dogs barkin'— *rrrworr, rrrworr, rrrworr*—I couldn't understand 'em."

"When I first come up here, couldn't nobody understand *me*," Abraham grinned. "They won't understand you neither!"

The two men laughed, and while Ladysmith wasn't sure she liked the joke, she laughed too. Abraham told how when he first got to Gettysburg, he was scared all the time. "I kept thinkin' the paterollers were gon' come get me and take me back in chains. For the longest time, every noise outside my house, I just knew I was done for."

"What's a pateroller?" Ladysmith asked.

"Mean men with mean dogs, who chase and catch runaway slaves," said Abraham. Then he said, "Lamar, tell me more about the ambulances. They got the same in the Union army?"

Chapter 3

Afterward, Abraham knew what he had to do. No point in tellin' himself he didn't, 'cause he did. That little thorn that was pesterin' him in his head had to be dealt with; he was going to have to join the Union army if they'd have him. This was his fight as much as anybody's.

Ladysmith finished the daisy chains she'd been making and put one around each of their necks and an extra long one around Charity's.

Abraham opened the tin that held his dinner. "You hungry?" he asked Lamar.

"Not so much today," he replied. "But I surely have been. Cornmeal mixed with water, and tough beef when you can get it, will kill you quicker'n a Yankee bullet. We did some better when we got up here."

Lamar rummaged through his haversack hoping to come up with something to add to the picnic. He had a spoon that he'd brought from home, half a bar of soap, a sewing kit called a "housewife," which he used for mending, and a clean pair of drawers with the seat neatly patched and mended. The only thing he had to share was a plug of tobacco that his sister had sent from home. Abraham shook his head when Lamar offered it. "I don't indulge," he said. "But thank you anyway."

Then the three of them shared biscuits, thick slices of bacon, and fresh tomatoes. Lamar and Abraham spoke of many things; the taste of fried okra eaten with deep fried bream, called "scrompers," scuppernong pie, made with sweet bronzy grapes, the song of a mockingbird at dawn, and the fragrant scent of honeysuckle on summer evenings.

Finishing a cherry tart, Lamar sighed contentedly. "That's the best meal I've had in months," he said. "I thank you kindly." Tears suddenly filled his eyes and he glanced away. "I tell you, Abraham, if I ever git home to live in peace, I am going to have plenty to eat that is good and nice."

The old tree sheltered them. Below, the meadow was

starred with wild flowers. In high summer the land was ripe with promise. Abraham wondered if there was anything fairer to look upon than fields of green. He glanced over at Lamar. There were things about each one that the other could never understand. But they had one thing in common; they loved the land they came from: Abraham in *spite* of who he was, and Lamar *because* of who he was.

"This here's mighty fair country," said Lamar.

"It is that," said Abraham, then he paused. "But it don't come up to home in my eyes."

Distant rifle fire popped sharp as firecrackers. Ladysmith looked up. The breeze that lifted the smoke from the hills played in her hair, blowing strands as fine as dandelion fluff.

Lamar rose, and Abraham lifted Ladysmith up onto Charity's back. Then they walked back to the fence.

"I expect this is farewell," said Lamar.

"I expect so," Abraham replied. "And I bid you farewell, indeed."

Chapter 4

On their way back, as they passed beneath the dappled shade of the trees, Abraham found himself still listening for something. Off in the distance, occasional picket fire sounded, as soldiers grew restless or bored. Overhead, he heard the fluting call of a redbird. But he was listening for something else; something he didn't yet hear.

"Abraham," said Ladysmith, interrupting his thoughts. "I been thinking about Lamar."

"Uh huh."

"Well," she said, "he said his feet were tough as a lightard knot. What's a lightard knot?"

Abraham chuckled. "It's a pinewood," he explained, "the red heart of it. Takes a heavy arm to cleave it with an ax. It's as strong as a heart's wish."

Ladysmith's mother was waiting for them at the paddock gate. "Did you see any soldiers?" she asked. "Mrs. Wills said there were Union troops up at the Seminary."

"Saw one rebel," said Abraham. "But they're all around. You can hear 'em breathin'." As he led Charity into the paddock, Ladysmith ran over and kissed the mule's soft muzzle.

"I wish you wouldn't kiss that mule," said her mother.

"I love her," said Ladysmith.

At twilight Abraham sat out on his front stoop. There was a fine mist in the air, so soft it scarcely felt like rain. In the surrounding hills, campfires flickered like fireflies. He could feel a great trembling, as though giant wings beat on the air, fanning invisible currents that quivered and shook. He was listening, but he didn't know for what. He recalled a song his mama used to sing, something about trembling:

Green trees are bending,
Poor sinners stand a-trembling;
The trumpet sounds within my soul,
I ain't got long to stay here.

Something terrible was about to happen and there was nothing he could do about it. Music wafted down through the gloom and then a chorus of men's voices . . . *"Be it ever so humble, there's no place like home . . ."*

He couldn't tell if the song was sung by Confederate or Union troops. But it was a sweet sound, causing him to ponder on the strangeness of the world. And how it happened that the first person he'd been able to really talk to in nearly four years was a white man and the enemy. As the song drifted away and disappeared, he got up and went into the barn. Charity turned dark eyes on him, trusting him.

"We might be takin' a little trip in the mornin'," he told her. "And we might, or we might not, have long to stay here." Then he went into his house and closed the door.

That evening, Ladysmith wrote a letter to her father who was with the Union army somewhere in Maryland:

Dear Father,
Today I met a Johnny Reb. He is tall and skinny and does not have any shoes. His name is Lamar. If you see him in battle somewhere, please do not shoot at him. He

is very nice. We have not seen any war yet, but there's troops here. We don't have any more sugar. And I hate molasses.
Your loving,
Ladysmith
P.S. If they are shooting at you, please stay low. Let the bullets go over your head. Mama is sending you some socks she made.

A few miles away, Lamar was writing to his sister, Pearl. A light rain had begun and he sat under the sheltering branches of a tree, bending into the lamplight. There was an air of goodwill, lightheartedness in the camp. Nearby, a man was hawking some kind of medicine. "Guaranteed to cure what ails you!" he vowed to two young recruits who stood listening to his promises. There was a smell of roasting meat in the air, and somewhere through the rain came the thin, reedy sound of a harmonica.

Dear Pearl,
I take pen in hand to write to you. I don't have anything to bear on to write so forgive the lines. This is the last good paper I have. My pen is a turkey feather and I do

not know how long it will last, but I will keep sharpening it. Pen points cost a dollar a piece and are scarce at that. We don't git but $11 a month for bein in the army. The ink is pokeberry, a fair pink to begin with but will fade. Real ink is too dear. One of the boys wrote this poem:

"My pen is bad, my ink is pale,
My love for you will never fail."

This should be told to a girlfriend, but since I don't have one you will have to do. The boys is cooking supper and some is playing cards. I have not had word from you in some while now. How is the crops? Write me ever particular, how high the corn is. How is old Blue? He misses huntin with me I know. How is my mule? I saw a fine mule here today belongs to a culler man who used to be a slave. He talked to me jest fine.

The wheat fields here looks like heaven's streets of gold. Please write to me. I feel mightily down when the mail comes and the others git letters and I don't, but it has not been that way often.

I remain yr brother,
Lamar

* * * *

Lamar enjoyed a hearty meal of roast beef, biscuits, and vegetables, and was grateful for the good food that raiding parties had brought back from the rich farmlands nearby. After supper he watched as some of the men played cards. Then he went to sleep.

At his house Abraham lay in the darkness listening to the tick of the clock that sounded like his own heartbeat. He knew what had irked him during his conversation with Lamar and he wouldn't ignore it. He would take action. The way he figured, it wasn't right for folks he didn't even know, white folks at that, to be fighting against slavery and he wasn't there to help.

'Course, it wasn't all his fault. At the start of the war, coloreds weren't *allowed* to fight. It was plain dumb, but there it was. But the United States Congress had changed that, and now they could. He didn't want anything to do with guns or shooting, but he could sure drive an ambulance wagon. After all, he had the finest mule in the country, in the North *or* South.

It was funny when Abraham thought about how he'd reached his decision to join the army: It had been Lamar, a rebel soldier, who had made him see the need to go off to battle.

Chapter 5

July 1, 1863

Abraham opened his eyes to the predawn chorus of birds outside his window. He got up from his bed and lit the oil lamp on the small table nearby. On it was a well-thumbed copy of a farmer's almanac that Mrs. Lightly had given him. It was a very helpful book. It told of the phases of the moon, the seasons, and when to plant:

> <u>July 1</u>—*Bush or Snap Beans*
> *Choose, at this season, a piece of ground in*
> *an open situation; let the ground be well*
> *dug, and laid even.*

It was July 1, and he'd already planted his snap beans, and had hoped to plant a second crop, but it didn't seem like he'd have time. Then he opened his Bible and read a verse as he did every morning of his life. He turned to Ecclesiastes:

> *To every thing there is a season, and a time*
> *to every purpose under the heaven: A time*
> *to be born, and a time to die; a time to plant,*
> *and a time to pluck up that which is planted.*

He continued to read. He was looking for something; a sign, something to tell him that he was doing the right thing:

> *Wherefore I perceive that there is nothing*
> *better, than that a man should rejoice in his*
> *own works; for that is his portion.*

His portion. Abraham thought about that. Perhaps what he was about to do *was* truly his work, and would be his portion. He hoped that his decision would please the Lord.

A few miles away from Abraham's house, a Confederate officer, Major General Henry Heth, was told about a warehouse full of shoes in Gettysburg. He wanted those shoes for his barefoot men. The rebel army was a walking army. But their long marches had used up the supply of leather and the South was unable to produce and furnish the needs of their foot soldiers. Heth asked permission to go into town with his men. "If there is no objection," he said.

"None in this world," replied his superior officer, A. P. Hill. Birdsong was still strong in the air as the men left camp and made their way toward town.

From the tower at the Lutheran Seminary, Brigadier General John Buford, a Kentuckian and Union officer, looked out over the town of Gettysburg and beyond at the land that was a series of ridges, like waves in the earth. A faint rain washed the valleys and hills in silver. It was a farmer's rain, gentle and soft. Then, taking up his binoculars, he spotted Major General Heth's troops as they came down the Chambersburg Pike. In a few moments the early morning quiet was shattered by gunfire. He sent word to General John Reynolds whose troops were six miles away. *Rebel infantry attacked at dawn. Expecting relief. John Buford.*

* * * *

Finishing his hot tea, Abraham fed Enoch, then packed himself a lunch. When he was ready to go, he looked around his cottage. His rocking chair sat next to the small table, which he'd made himself, that held his mama's sewing basket. When the old clock chimed seven times, he put the cat out and the latch on, closed the door, then went out to the barn for Charity. He walked out into a cool, misty rain.

He stopped by to tell Mrs. Lightly that he was on his way to Union headquarters to join the ambulance corps. She'd been up since dawn, baking bread. The town had been warned that fierce fighting could take place that day, in or around Gettysburg. General John Reynolds had sent word suggesting that civilians stay indoors, and in cellars if possible. He was particularly concerned about the children.

"Charity and me, well, it's like we been called," Abraham told Mrs. Lightly, accepting two loaves of freshly baked bread for his journey. "Please take care of Enoch for me. And if something should happen to me, I'd like for Ladysmith to have my mama's basket."

"No!" said Ladysmith, coming in the kitchen. "Don't go, they'll shoot you!" She ran into his arms.

He hugged her for a moment, then gently released her.

"Ain't nobody gon' shoot me," he said. "If I've come this far, I don't expect anybody's aimin' for me now." Then he took his leave, turning to look back once. Ladysmith was standing out in the road, waving good-bye.

After Abraham had left, Mrs. Lightly stood in the kitchen, trying to collect her thoughts. "Get your things together," she told Ladysmith, who'd come back inside and was looking out of the window to where Abraham had disappeared down the road. "We're going down to the cellar till the fighting's over." She began gathering lanterns, filling them with oil and trimming the wicks. Then she went to fetch a pail for fresh water.

Ladysmith rushed up to her room, and a minute later rushed back down again. "Enoch!" she cried. "I've got to find Enoch!" And she dashed out of the back door to look for the cat.

Out on the Cashtown Road, Lamar was eating breakfast. The food was good, even eaten in the rain. It was a far cry from the fare the troops had been getting all these months. *Pennsylvania is rich land,* he thought, and again, raiding parties had done a fine job of providing the best food the surrounding countryside had to offer. He ate heartily of flapjacks, ham, and apple butter, and enjoyed the first real coffee he'd had in months. Until they'd come north, the men had been drinking a vile mixture brewed from parched corn, peanuts, and dried apples. The only resemblance it bore to coffee was the color.

"Our thanks to the state of Pennsylvania," said the man sitting next to him, lifting his precious cup of coffee in a mock toast.

The tinny sound of a band floated over the camp. Finishing his meal, Lamar walked over to the road to watch the musicians. Down the way he saw a sight that fair lifted his heart. General Robert E. Lee was heading toward them on his tall, dapple-gray horse, Traveler. Troops were gathering along the fence, watching him. A few moved close, reaching out tentative hands to touch the horse. Lee smiled slightly, as if embarrassed by the attention. He raised an arm in salute and removed his soft black hat. The sun broke through the clouds, burnishing his silver hair. Tears rushed to Lamar's eyes so that the general appeared as a figure in a book, misty and outlined in light. Then an officer rode close to the fence, urging the men back. The band struck up the lively strains of "Dixie."

Lamar was so excited about seeing the general in person that he went back to write a quick letter to Pearl.

Dear Pearl,
I seat myself down one time more to let you know that I am in the best of health. I had to tell you what happened today. I saw ole Bobby Lee. The general in person. I don't talk fancy like some others, but I tell you it was like lookin at an angel. His hair was shining in the sun and he looked so fine. Somebody said that while he was sleepin an entire unit passed by his tent and tippy-toed so's not to waken him.

Gen Longstreet will be leading my way to battle this day. I don't aim to worry you none but Doc Fairlie's been busy settin up the field hospital for the wounded. I reckon I should be fearful of what's ahead but Gen Lee never let us down yet. We'll be marching in a little while. Whatever happens I'll try to make you proud of me.
Yr faithful brother,
Lamar

Rain dripped from the trees onto the brim of Abraham's old straw hat. He felt like he was riding into the eye of a storm. In the dense fog nothing was familiar; the landscape seemed strange and sinister. Charity's hoofbeats were muffled and thick. He thought about what Ladysmith had said about his getting shot. But somehow, he just didn't believe he would be. Something else worried him, though. He knew that some of the whites and most of the blacks in the area had left for fear of being captured by the rebels. He wasn't sure what happened to white prisoners, but he knew that blacks would be sent south and back into slavery if they were caught. He figured he'd heap rather be shot than caught.

When he reached the outskirts of town, the sun broke through buttermilk skies, burning off the fog and promising a hot day. As he drew nearer, there was a rattle of gunfire, then the distant booming of cannonade. Suddenly, a high, thin wailing seemed to rise up out of the earth. Charity pricked up her ears and came to a dead halt. Goosebumps peppered Abraham's arms and the hairs rose on the back of his neck. The sound was eerie, like a giant animal in pain; but not a real animal, something imagined, something dreaded only in dreams. It was the most terrifying sound he'd ever heard.

At the same time Abraham heard it, John Buford heard it up in the tower of the Seminary. Only he *knew* what it was—the rebel yell—issuing from a thousand throats as they attacked. The rebels were moving rapidly eastward, down the Chambersburg Pike until they topped a rise. There, they met Buford's troops and came under Union fire.

At 8:30, John Reynolds arrived with his troops. He was a man much admired by both armies. Most men believed he was the best general in the Union army. He moved his men toward McPherson's Ridge where they engaged Heth's Confederate troops. Heavy fighting ensued. By midafternoon, the Confederates had beaten the Union troops, forcing them south of town to Cemetery Hill. There, Union forces held the high ground. John Reynolds lay dead from a sniper's bullet.

The cellar smelled of dust and apples. Dragging her quilt, and carrying Enoch in her arms, Ladysmith made her way across the big, shadowy room. Her mother lit the lantern and placed it on the wooden table against one wall. In its light, jars of homemade jellies and pre-serves that lined the shelves glowed like stained glass. Ladysmith glanced around nervously. She was positive there were spiders nearby and she was scared of spiders. She could practically feel them crawling on the back of her neck. Reaching back, she touched a spiderweb and jumped. "I hate it down here," she said.

The first roar of cannon shook the house, and sent dust down from the walls and ceiling. Ladysmith held on to Enoch for dear life. His ears were back and his thick tail twitched nervously. She put her hands over her ears and scooted under the table with him.

"They've got no right to do this!" she exclaimed. "We haven't done anything!"

Her mother tried to calm her. "Maybe it won't last long," she said. "We might even go back upstairs to sleep tonight."

But Ladysmith wasn't having any of it. She was terrified, and there was nobody to help them. Her daddy was off at war, Abraham had deserted them, and here they were, just waiting to get blown away. Another fierce cannonade shook the house and Ladysmith curled up in the quilt, pulling it close over her head. Then she said her prayers.

At 5:50 that afternoon, the guns on both sides grew still. Confederate troops were busy capturing Union fugitives out of cellars and alleys in the town. Abraham, who had remained hidden in the woods until the fighting in his area ended, now made his way to Union headquarters.

This fight on July 1 had begun over shoes. But the decisions made by junior officers of both armies, had committed their commanding generals—Lee on the Confederate side, and Meade on the Union—to a battle at Gettysburg. It had not been Lee's intent to fight there. But as the battle unfolded, and appeared to be a Confederate victory, he said to General Longstreet, "They [the Union troops] are there in position, and I am going to whip them or they are going to whip me."

Chapter 6

July 2, 1863

The next morning Abraham found himself south of town, in a field where large boulders crouched like animals turned to stone. He'd been looking for field headquarters most of the morning. Campfires were scattered about under gray skies. Fog covered the ground. A Union soldier pointed toward an officer standing near an open tent.

"Talk to Colonel Chamberlain," he said.

The colonel was tall with a tawny mustache. His uniform trousers were rumpled and he wore a three-foot sword. When he greeted Abraham, he was mannerly, and if he was surprised to see an old colored man with his mule, he gave no indication of it. Instinctively, Abraham felt that he was someone to be trusted. They spoke for a moment, then Chamberlain scratched something on a card and handed it to Abraham. "You don't need to go to headquarters," he said. Then he directed him to the field hospital.

The field hospital had been set up behind Union lines. When he got there, Abraham reported to a sergeant who seemed to be in charge.

"I'm here to join the army," he said.

"You're too old," said the man, who had a red face and a gruff manner.

"I don't believe so," said Abraham. "I ain't too old to drive a mule."

The sergeant looked up from the table where he was writing something. "Somebody send you?" he asked, really looking at Abraham for the first time.

"Gentleman by the name of Chamberlain," replied Abraham.

The man looked surprised. "*Colonel* Chamberlain?"

"Yessir," replied Abraham, handing him the bit of paper the colonel had given him.

Reading the note, the sergeant asked, "That your mule over there?"

"Yessir," Abraham said again. "Name's Charity."

"Well, congratulations," said the sergeant. "You are now in the ambulance corps."

A few minutes later Abraham was given a blue cap and a canvas cover for his wagon. He wasn't really in the army, they explained later, but he would serve as an ambulance driver, picking up the wounded from the battlefield and bringing them back to the field hospital.

Lamar had been marching since before dawn. Now he waited with the rest of his unit in Longstreet's First Corps. They'd marched and countermarched most of the day. *It was strange,* he thought, looking out over the valley below. *Even though all of Lee's army was out there somewhere, no one was to be seen.* The Yanks were out there too. He could feel them breathing, feel them waiting. But only the grass moved, and the leaves of the trees.

Now, in late afternoon, they stood in deep shade, looking out over a flat green rise up toward the Emmitsburg Road. Beyond that, to the south, were two hills, Big Round Top and Little Round Top. The Union army was dug in along the crests of both hills—in possession of the high ground.

The sun was burning, white hot, the hottest day of the year. In the shade of the trees, the men were quiet, waiting for their orders. Hoofbeats thudded softly as a solitary horse moved behind them. Through the dappled shade, Lamar saw Longstreet's black Irish stallion. There was a murmur among the men. Their general, "Old Pete," was close by. They loved and trusted him and would fight their last good fight for him.

Way off, a band was playing "Dixie," but they were playing it slow, not as a bright, spritely march but like a hymn. Lamar had never before heard it played in quite that way. Leaves rustled overhead. A redbird called. The men stayed in the woods for an hour and seven minutes. Then, the orders came. The unit stepped from the shelter of the trees and out into the open field and the bright, bright light. Guns went off, one by one, growing to one long, terrible explosion that went on and on. Then, Union fire began, the first shells falling through the trees.

Lamar's ears rang with the horrific noise. He stepped out into the field, the smell of grass and smoke caught in his throat. It was as though he moved in a vacuum; his hearing was gone. It was like being underwater. The bright light seemed to hold him, covering him like a cape. Time stood still. Yet he could feel the grass against his feet and the heat pulsing against his face.

Waves of dust rose from the feet of all those men and drifted into the shining air like clouds. Bright flags of red and blue rippled in the hot breeze. A standard bearer marched forward carrying the flag. In an instant he was shot, and before the flag hit the ground, it was gathered into the arms of another soldier. Lamar saw the man next to him fall, but it was as though he fell in silence. Then a terrible explosion ripped through the line and he watched, amazed, as an entire row of men disappeared.

The musket ball's heat raced across Lamar's face with the shock of lightning. He fell forward, his left arm useless under him. He didn't feel pain so much as a deadening numbness, like he'd been given an awful jolt. Then, he was struck again. A minié ball pierced his thigh, fairly lifting him off the ground. *Oh, no,* he thought, *oh, no.* Then, conscious only of great heat and monstrous noise, he fell, and was swallowed up in darkness.

In these last two days of fighting, Union and Confederate armies had suffered 35,000 dead, wounded, or captured—more than ten times the number of people then living in the entire town of Gettysburg.

Through the rest of the day and into the evening, Lamar lay in an open field, sometimes gaining, sometimes losing consciousness. When he was awake, he thought about home and the people he loved. He thought about Pearl and about his dog, Blue. And about the mountains wreathed in mist, fold on fold, in hues of violet and blue. He didn't want to die alone and was afraid that no one from his regiment would be able to find him in the dark.

The sun was setting. He opened his eyes and heard a terrible sound. It was a strange, mournful noise that seemed to come up out of the earth. The moaning went on and on and then he thought, *Oh, dear Lord . . . that's my own voice I hear.* And how was it he was so cold? He was colder than he'd ever been in his life. Colder than snow, colder than ice. And so thirsty. Closing his eyes, he thought of cool mountain streams rushing over smooth stones. He cried out again, his cries mingling with the cries from the others who lay on the ground. Then he heard something else—a footfall. Moving his head slightly, he saw the boots and trousers of a Union uniform.

"Reb?" said a distant voice. "Can you hold up your head?"

The soldier in blue knelt beside Lamar in the thin twilight.

"Here," he said, holding his canteen up to Lamar's

lips. Lamar drank gratefully of the warmish water, and when he could speak, asked, "What you doin' out here among the dead?"

"Lookin' for my brother," replied the young soldier. "He's a reb too."

"I pray you find him well," murmured Lamar.

Charity and Abraham moved among the dead and dying on the field. Tattered bits of cloths trembled in a faint breeze, giving a false impression of living things. Dead horses were piled in mounds. Looking down from the wagon, Abraham saw a severed horse's foot. His stomach churned and bile rose up in his throat.

Men from both sides moved across the field, searching out the wounded. The bottom parts of their bodies were hidden by the smoke that drifted low over the ground. The sound of men's moans rose and fell in waves. Then Abraham knew what he'd been listening for in the time before the battle. Now he heard it: It was the sound of death.

"Lord God," he prayed softly. "Help us to help them."

Moving slowly forward, Charity seemed to know what to do—how to find the living. She made a soft, snuffling sound and paused at a fallen boy. Nuzzling his face, she then lifted her head: There was no breath in him. She moved on.

"Whoooaa," Abraham said softly.

Charity halted, looked down. Saw a poor man who had died. She looked back at Abraham.

"Over there," he said, nudging her forward.

There was something familiar about the fallen soldier. Even in the gathering dusk, even beneath the blood, he thought he recognized the boy. Charity moved closer.

Warm breath misted lightly, and Lamar felt something tickle his face. He opened his eyes, expecting to see the wings of the Angel of Death. Instead, soft brown eyes peered into his, and Charity gave a soft snuffle.

"Lamar?" said Abraham softly, getting down from the wagon. "How you?"

"Tolerable," Lamar replied weakly. "But jes' barely."

"You' gon' be fine," said Abraham. "We'll get you some doctorin'." He knew that Lamar would want to be brought to the Confederate field hospital for help, but he was afraid to take him. In order to do that, he and Charity would have to cross Confederate lines. And while he didn't think anybody was much concerned about a solitary colored man bearing a wounded rebel, or if they'd even pay any attention to him, he was scared to take the chance. He might never get back. Some fool man just might get it in his head to send Abraham back south. He looked at Lamar lying so still and helpless, and his own heart wrenched with sadness.

"Come on, Charity," he said softly. "We gone' take this boy back to our side. They'll take care of him."

Chapter 7

July 3, 1863

Abraham heard a mockingbird, its song like liquid silver falling on the air. Then he opened his eyes and knew that he'd been dreaming. There were no birdcalls in that place. It was just before dawn, and he was lying on the ground next to his wagon at the edge of the Union field hospital. Stiffly, his old joints creaking, he pulled himself up by the wagon wheel.

There was a faint smell of decay over the field. In the largest tent, surgeons were operating by candlelight. They'd been working throughout the night, and the stack of amputated limbs outside the tent had grown larger, some of the legs with the shoes and stockings still on them. Everywhere he looked, there were men lying on the ground, some dead, some near death. Lamar was there somewhere, but Lord only knew where. Abraham groaned. *Surely this has to end soon,* he thought, leading Charity down to the creek for water. But by all accounts, today would be another battle, and he would go back to gather up what wounded still lived on the battlefield.

In early morning Mrs. Lightly stood up and shook out the folds of her dress. The cellar was shadowy and cool. "Do you hear anything?" she asked.

Ladysmith, still sleepy, listened intently for the sound of guns. "*I* don't. Do you think it's over?"

"I sincerely hope so," replied her mother. "And even if it isn't, we need to go back upstairs for food and water."

"And fresh air," said Ladysmith, who was beginning to feel like a mole.

They had started up the steps when a creaking sound stopped them in their tracks. Someone was walking around upstairs! There was the heavy tread of boots moving from the front of the house to the back. Easing back down the steps, Ladysmith and her mother hid in the shadows in the farthest corner of the cellar.

* * * *

The red blossoms of poppies stippled the golden fields of wheat. Long silences were broken only by the whisper of wind. The Confederates looked across the Peach Orchard, a patch of woods, and those gleaming empty fields and up toward Cemetery Ridge. There, Union troops waited.

Then came the words that would change the face of the war. Longstreet, who believed Lee's plans for that day's battle could only end in disaster for his men, nevertheless gave the orders: "Let the batteries open!"

The hot afternoon stillness was shattered when, at 1:07 P.M., cannons began going off, one by one by one, growing to a long, continuous firing of what was the heaviest cannonade ever heard on American soil.

Approximately 11,000 soldiers made up the Confederate assault force that day. Major General George Pickett prepared to lead his three brigades— 4,900 men—across those wheat fields and a mile of open terrain up toward Cemetery Ridge. On the Union side, General Winfield Scott Hancock waited with his three divisions, roughly 13,000 men.

When Pickett's Charge, as the battle was called, ended an hour and a half later, 7,500 men had been killed, wounded, or captured. The total casualties for the

Union infantry was 1,500, just a fraction of the number they inflicted while maintaining their position. As it became apparent to Union troops, even before the final guns were halted, that the battle was theirs, a wild celebration broke out on the heights.

Down below, the Confederates straggled slowly back across a bloody plain. General Lee rode out to meet them. "It is all my fault," he told the men. "It is all my fault." Those who could, took off their hats to him. Then they drifted on, dragging their muskets behind them, melding like shades into the deep hollows and folds of the hills.

Later, the true total of Lee's losses in Pennsylvania would be nearly 28,000 men. All told, over three bloody days, more than 50,000 men, both blue and gray, had been killed, wounded, or captured.

At sunset, when the guns finally grew quiet, Ladysmith and her mother crawled out from under the table and made their way up the stairs, not knowing what awaited them. Shakily, they stepped up into a house that they barely recognized. Pale and wan from their hours underground, they blinked at the light of the setting sun that shone through the open front door. The smell of gunpowder was acrid and sharp. They walked through shadowy rooms where windowpanes were cracked and broken. There were bullet holes in some of the walls, and the floors were caked with dry mud. Living room curtains hung awry over windows open to the outside. Evidence that someone had foraged in the house was plain.

"Deserters!" whispered Ladysmith's mother. "That's who we heard. Only deserters could have had the time to plunder. They're despicable." Cautiously, she tiptoed into the hall, keeping Ladysmith behind her. But the house was quiet, not with a waiting stillness, but a finished one.

In the kitchen the pantry had been plundered and the pie safe emptied. Bits of broken crockery spilled across the table and onto the floor. The back door, too, was wide open.

Ladysmith stood with her back against the wall. She'd been so scared that even the hairs on her arms hurt. She felt dirty and gritty. "Let's look upstairs," whispered her mother. Though afraid, Ladysmith followed her mother up the steps. They peeked into Mrs. Lightly's room. Her writing desk and chest had been looted, the drawers thrown about by someone possibly looking for silver or jewelry.

Ladysmith went slowly into her own room. Except for a few bullet holes, it looked the same as when she had left it. She remembered how things used to be before the battle, when she could read by the lamplight. Sometimes she and her mother would have hot cocoa in the kitchen and maybe Enoch would come for a visit and a small treat. Now, everything had changed.

Suddenly, there was a slight movement from beneath her bed. She screamed and jumped back. Enoch crept out, the pupils of his eyes black as coals. Shakily, she picked him up. Unbeknownst to her, he'd followed her to her room as quietly as a shadow, as anxious as she to escape imprisonment in the cellar.

They discovered that the barn was not badly damaged, and while the animals had evidently been frightened by the noise and smoke, only one cow was missing. Abraham's house had also been plundered, and a tree in his front garden had been shattered by gunfire. There were numerous bullet holes in his walls too.

The moon was rising when they went out to the front porch. The air was hot and damp and felt like rain, and an unearthly stillness engulfed them. Smoke hung in the branches of the trees in a pearly mist. Not a bird called. They had no idea if the Union or the Confederacy had won that day's battle—if it was over for good, or just for the day.

But Lamar knew. He was now a prisoner of war and had been moved to the Lutheran church in town. Along with him were fifty other wounded rebels who'd been captured when the area around the Confederate field hospital had been overtaken by Union troops. All of the churches, and every other large building in Gettysburg, were now occupied by Union forces, and pressed into use as hospitals. He was only semiconscious when he was taken inside the church where soldiers lay on long pews and in every aisle.

The next day, Independence Day, rain began falling on Gettysburg. At first, just a drizzle, then the heavens seemed to open up and pound the land. Water fell in torrents, filling trenches and flooding streams where men lay on the banks, helpless and dying. It washed the blood from the grass and the stones and the faces of the dead.

When it became evident that General Meade was not going to attack, the Confederates made plans to leave Gettysburg. All hope that Robert E. Lee had of invading the North had ended. At noon the wounded began being loaded onto ambulances. Most of the rickety wagons had no springs and very little straw to cushion the ride. Then the ambulance wagon train began hauling the injured and dying over rutted roads for the long journey southward. The train was seventeen miles long.

In Gettysburg alone, nearly 10,000 men were on their way to northern or southern prisons. And 7,000 bodies needed to be buried. There were 34,000 wounded men in the area.

Lamar was lucky. He was faring as well as could be expected. At least he was out of the rain.

Chapter 8

August 1863

Abraham was on his way home. Charity plodded slowly down the road. From the fields on either side of them came the stench of dead and rotting bodies of horses still unburied. Abraham was tired and heartsick, but he knew that he and Charity had done good work. He'd stayed on as an ambulance driver after the battle. His latest job had been to take patients from hospitals to the railroad station.

A week earlier, on a hot, scorching day, he'd driven a wagon full of soldiers down to the station. There, they could take a train to Baltimore and from there to wherever their families waited. Clouds of dust rose from the road, coating buildings and what fences remained with a thin layer of grime. He passed a group of soldiers walking in the heat and dust, helped along by other walking wounded. He'd have picked them up, but he had no more room in the wagon. Just then, a farmer driving his own wagon passed them by, causing them to move over to the side of the road. He carried only one passenger.

It made Abraham so mad he could hardly stand it. Why hadn't the man picked up some of the soldiers on the road? It didn't make any sense to him, and when he got to the station, he told another driver about what he'd seen. The driver held up his hand and made a hard fist.

"These farmers!" He spat out the words angrily. "They're hard as a fist." He told Abraham that some of the local men were making a name for themselves by their stinginess. "They been chargin' those poor soldiers, who got wounded *defending* the farmers' very land, to drive them to the station. Most soldiers got no money at all. Ought to be a law agin' it," he said angrily.

When Abraham returned to the hospital, he told the doctor in charge of surgery about it, and the government sent some men from the provost marshal's office to investigate. It was hard to believe that some folks could be so unkind. But for all of that, Abraham still believed that there were more kind people than unkind people. For instance, just as soon as the railroad started running again, after the tracks were repaired, ladies began arriving from all over to help with the wounded. Seemed like in no time the hospitals were cleaner, food was prepared better, and the poor soldiers got better treatment. He figured it was a woman's war, well as a man's.

Charity began moving a bit faster. She recognized home. Abraham sat up a bit straighter. He said a small prayer that home would still be there, and that everything and everybody he loved would be fine. He looked at the back of Charity's head and felt such a surge of affection for her that he had to take a deep breath to keep from crying.

Lamar called softly to the nurse as she came down the aisle with a stack of fresh linen.

"Ma'am?" he inquired.

He lay on a hard pew in the church hospital, but he did have a quilt under him to soften his bed. His wounds had been washed and dressed, but he had no use of his left arm or leg. "I was wonderin', could you get me some writin' paper? I need to let Pearl know I'm not dead."

"Can you write it yourself?" she asked.

He misunderstood her, saying, "Oh yes, ma'am. I can write pretty good. Not too good at spellin', though."

"I meant, can you use your hand?"

"Yes'm," he replied. "My right one's fine."

After she left, leaving him with a pen and a few pieces of paper, he pushed a corner of the quilt away, and bearing on the pew, began his letter.

Dear Pearl,

I take pen in hand to write to let you know I am not dead. I am writing on Yankee paper with a Yankee pen and I am in a Yankee hospital. I got hit in the left arm and my leg. I expect I'll be here for a while.

That battle was a turrible thang. My last day out, shells was so thick I felt like I could reach out and catch them in my hat. That last day was even worse. Leastways, more died. Somebody said Robert E. Lee come to the men when it was over and said it was all his fault. It wasn't though. We failed him. The Yankees held the high ground. We couldn't fight up them hills.

You recall I told you bout the colored man with the mule I met. Abraham Small by name. Well he found me hurt on the field and took me to a Yankee field hospital. He saved my life.

I still don't feel too good. I miss home like a fire in my bones. Theres not much I wouldn't give to come home. I want to see those mountains all blue with mist. And go down to the holler where the water in the creek is clear as glass. Our home is plain but I surely would love to see it again. The kitchen with its puncheon floor, even the corn crib with cracks unstopped. You been a good sister to me and I feel I did not say. Now I do.

What I wish is you would send some okra seed to A. Small, c/o M. Litely who he works for to plant in spring. When I get home I believe I will plant cotton as the boys say it will be scarce as hens teeth when the war is over. Also, if you could send me some cane syrup made on the place, I would be happy. You can send it here, to the church.

I tell you one thing, if war comes around again, I ain't gone be there.

Yr. Loving bro,
Lamar

Chapter 9

Autumn, 1863

Over the previous weeks, there'd been a change in the sunlight. It grew mellow and golden, and kinder than the summer's sun. Abraham and Ladysmith had gathered windfall apples; yellow, green, and red. This year, the reds seemed redder but perhaps it was just a trick of the light. It was the time of year when everything dropped onto the earth, from apples to chestnuts.

Abraham and Ladysmith were in his garden. He had taken down an apple tree that was old and no longer bearing. He rubbed his hands over the wood with pleasure; it was good, and would be fragrant and long burning. Charity waited patiently as he loaded the logs into the back of the wagon. Even though she couldn't say, she seemed happy to be home again.

Ladysmith was sitting up on the seat of the wagon. She wore a rose-colored shawl and her cheeks were the same bright pink. "Sure wish we knew what happened to Lamar," she said.

Abraham finished loading the wood into the wagon. "I hope he's back home by now," he said.

That evening, Ladysmith and her mother were having dinner with Mr. and Mrs. David Wills. Over dessert of apple pie, Mr. Wills told them about his idea.

"I'd like to make our cemetery a *national* one," he said. "After all, this battle was perhaps the most crucial of the war." His dark eyes were eager. He told them he'd bought seventeen acres next to the cemetery and had hired a landscape architect to design the new burial ground. "If my plan works, we'll have a dedication ceremony."

The ladies had been listening attentively. Ladysmith finally asked, "What's the difference between a regular cemetery and a *national* one?"

"That's a good question, young lady," replied Mr. Wills. He explained that a national cemetery would be maintained by the federal government. "For the men who served honorably for their country."

On a bleak November afternoon, a packet arrived for Abraham, sent in Mrs. Lightly's care. It was about the size of a small envelope, and was wrapped in burlap sacking, tied with twine. The little package was so frayed that it seemed a miracle that it had made it from the South to the North at all. And how it had come was a miracle in itself. It had left Rabun Gap by way of Lamar's cousin who was home on unofficial leave (he was homesick). When he returned to his company, he passed the package along to another soldier, who in turn sent it to a brother who was serving in the Union army. The little packet continued on through Union lines, soldier by soldier, until it reached Pennsylvania.

Mrs. Lightly looked at the faded ink of the return address and knew that the sender had tendered it with extreme faith. Ladysmith offered to take it to Abraham. "Come right back, now," her mother said. "Dinner's nearly ready. And wear your shawl, it's damp out."

While Ladysmith watched, Abraham sat in his rocking chair, and with careful hands, unwrapped the first mail he'd ever received.

Inside the rough sacking was a smaller packet and a letter. Opening the letter, he read:

Dear Mr. Small,
It is with sad heart that I tell you my brother, Lamar, has
passed from this earth. The letter telling me said he was
brave and did not complain one time. He wrote me to
send you some okra seeds, which I have done. I thank
you kindly for taking him to the doctors. You done the
best you could. Lamar passed from his wounds in battle
and a weakness in his chest. I know he is with the angels
now.
In sorrow, I ever remain,
Pearl Cooper

After comforting Ladysmith, and sending her back to
her mother, Abraham opened the small brown twist of
okra seeds. He poured them out and held them cupped
in the palm of his hand. The dull green seeds were round
as shot and felt faintly dusty, as though still warmed by
the southern sun. He put them back into the packet.
He'd plant them in spring when things looked more
hopeful.

Enoch got up from in front of the fire and came over
to him, his dark tail like a plume of smoke. Abraham
rubbed the cat's velvety head. Then he spoke words like
a small prayer.

"Fare thee well, Lamar," he said gently, "Fare thee very well indeed."

Firelight cast flickering shadows against the walls of David Wills's study. An oil lamp spilled gold across the surface of his desk. "Ladysmith," he said softly, looking up from the paper he was writing. "Are you awake?"

Ladysmith, who was keeping Mr. Wills company while her mother and Mrs. Wills sewed in the back parlor, gazed at him from the deep hollow of the big chair next to the hearth. In her lap was a black cat whose purring could be heard over the crackle of the fire. "Sir?" she said, coming back from her daydream.

"I have something to show you," he said.

Putting the cat down, she went over to his chair. On the desk in front of her was an invitation, the ink not yet dry.

"It's for President Lincoln," said Mr. Wills. "Asking him to say a few words at the dedication."

Ladysmith looked at the invitation written in Mr. Wills's slanting handwriting in thick black ink. It was dated November 2, 1863, and was addressed:

To His Excellency,
A. Lincoln,
President of the United States

"Can I tell Abraham?" she asked.

"You may," said Mr. Wills, smiling at her.

Ladysmith knew how happy Abraham would be. After all, he'd wanted Mr. Lincoln to be invited from the beginning. They had talked about it earlier when they learned that Mr. Edward Everett, the former governor of Massachusetts and secretary of state, had been invited as the main speaker at the ceremony. Abraham had shaken his head. "Should have asked Mr. Lincoln to speak," he'd said.

The president did receive an invitation, but only two weeks before the dedication, nearly six weeks after Mr. Everett had been invited. Someone later said that inviting the president had been an afterthought.

The day before the president was due to arrive, Abraham showed up at the Wills's back door. "I brought some wood for Mr. Lincoln," he said. "It's all I have to give him, but it's good wood and will burn proper." Then he stacked half a cord of his prized applewood in the woodpile and went on his way.

Chapter 10

November 18–19, 1863

The same pale evening star that Abraham had almost wished upon shone down on the train station as the four-car special from Washington arrived in Gettysburg just after sundown. Steam rose around the president's car that was brightly decorated with red, white, and blue bunting.

Mr. Lincoln and the dignitaries who'd come with him stepped from the train to the platform, and were surrounded by the crowd. Dressed in black, the president stood taller than anyone else, his angular figure rising like a lighthouse above the waves. A brass band struck up a march as he was ushered to the carriage that would take him to the Wills's residence.

The town was filled to overflowing with people

who'd come for the dedication ceremony. Military bands played and street musicians brightened every corner. When he reached the Wills's house, Mr. Lincoln was surrounded by a group of serenaders who stopped him on the front porch. Unwilling to make a speech before he'd had time to greet his hosts, the president nevertheless said a few words to the crowd.

"In my position, it is sometimes important that I should not say foolish things." Then from the back of the crowd someone said, "If you can help it."

The president smiled, his dark, craggy face brightening as though a lamp had been lit behind his eyes. "It very often happens that the only way to *help* it is to say nothing at all. Believing that is my present condition this evening, I must beg of you to excuse me from addressing you further."

Inside, Mr. and Mrs. Wills waited anxiously for Mr. Lincoln. Everything had been planned down to the last detail. Ladysmith had been promised that she would be able to greet the president and she had been waiting for him for what seemed like hours. But as is usual when things are too planned, nothing worked the way it was supposed to.

Mr. Edward Everett and Governor Curtin, who'd been

invited to dine with the president, arrived by carriage and were shown into the house. Then the other dignitaries showed up and in no time, the house was filled with people milling about, greeting one another as politicians will. Ladysmith found herself surrounded by big men in tuxedos who looked like so many penguins. She began to feel too warm. The scent of flowers and the smell of food caught in her throat. Suddenly she felt sick. Threading her way through the hall, she ran through the kitchen where strangers were preparing food, out the back door, and into the garden where she threw up in the hedge. Her mother found her there and took her home.

In the Wills's dining room, the table was beautifully set with fine china and silver. Crystal vases were filled with scarlet hothouse roses and fragrant white lilies. The floors had been polished until they shone with reflected firelight. When he entered the dining room, Mr. Lincoln went over to the fireplace where Abraham's applewood was burning cheerily. "I love an open fire," he told David Wills. "I always had one at home."

After dinner and then talk around the table, Mr. Lincoln excused himself and gathered up his papers. Taking a copy of his speech for the following day, he went next door to meet with Secretary of State William

Henry Seward, who'd come with him from Washington. When he returned to the house, about midnight, he went up to bed. From down in the hollow, Abraham watched Mr. Lincoln's light.

The next morning dawned cool and a bit overcast. Crowds gathered to await the arrival of the president for the march to Cemetery Hill. Some said more than 20,000 people had come for the dedication. Marching in the parade were members of the Union army and navy, a regiment of troops, hospital corps, military bands, Knights Templars, Masonic fraternity and other civilian organizations, the fire department, many dignitaries, and the press.

Abraham started out early to find the hospital corps, but the crowds were so large that he lost his bearings. Bands played military music, hawkers sold toffee and souvenirs, and all around him was a sea of people. He stopped close to a snake-rail fence and stood up in the wagon to get a better look. Nearby, a group of men in fine blue uniforms of the Union army waited to join the parade. Their horses, thoroughbreds all, were skittish and hard to hold. One officer, on an Arabian stallion that pranced nervously, looked over at Abraham and his mule. He said something to his friends who laughed and turned to look.

"Looks to me like the bottom rail doesn't know it belongs on the bottom," he said scornfully. "Old man, you'd best go to the end of the parade or back where you came from. You and that sorry-looking mule don't belong here."

But Abraham just turned away. He'd discovered early on that some folks were prejudiced, no matter what part of the country they came from. And that people were either kind, or they were not. "It don't matter what some folks say," he said softly, rubbing Charity's long ears. "We earned the right to be here, and we're gon' see President Lincoln and listen to the speechifying *no matter what*!"

Just then, a ripple of excitement passed through the crowd. Off in the distance, President Lincoln was coming up the road riding a beautiful chestnut horse that was reportedly the largest in the Cumberland Valley. In his black suit, stovepipe hat, and white gloves, the president appeared larger than life.

The parade only took fifteen minutes to reach Cemetery Hill. It was eleven o'clock, but Mr. Everett had not yet arrived. So the bands played and choirs sang and the crowd milled about until noon. Abraham and Charity went over to a small copse of trees to wait for the ceremony to begin. Beyond were the meadows, the orchards, and in the distance, wheat fields. Then Mr. Everett arrived, shook hands with the president, and greeted the other dignitaries on the platform. The U.S. House chaplain, the Reverend Thomas Stockton, offered a prayer. Mr. Everett was introduced. He rose, bowed to Mr. Lincoln, saying, "Mr. President." Mr. Lincoln responded, "Mr. Everett." Then, after gazing out over the fields and the crowd, Mr. Everett began:

As my eye ranges over the fields whose sods were so lately moistened by the blood of gallant and loyal men, I feel, as never before, how truly it was said of old that it is sweet and becoming to die for one's country.

He then gave an outline of how the war began and talked about the three-day battle at Gettysburg. All told, he spoke for two hours, which was not unusual in those days. Ending his speech, he said:

In the glorious annals of our common country, there will be no brighter page than that which relates to the Battle of Gettysburg.

Applause, sounding like pebbles thrown against a window pane, woke Abraham, who had begun to doze. Then the Baltimore Glee Club sang a song written for the occasion.

In the brief silence that followed, Abraham watched as Mr. Lincoln stood up, walked to the podium, took a paper from his coat pocket, and put on his steel-rimmed glasses. The breeze freshened, scattering fallen leaves over the ground and lifting a dark strand of Mr. Lincoln's hair. Abraham cupped one hand behind his ear, so as not to miss a single word.

Four score and seven years ago our fathers brought forth on this continent a new nation, conceived in liberty, and dedicated to the proposition that all men are created equal.

Now we are engaged in a great civil war, testing whether that nation, or any nation so conceived and so dedicated, can long endure. We are met on a great battle-

field of that war. We have come to dedicate a portion of that field, as a final resting place for those who here gave their lives that that nation might live. It is altogether fitting and proper that we should do this.

But, in a larger sense, we can not dedicate—we can not consecrate—we can not hallow—this ground. The brave men, living and dead, who struggled here have consecrated it, far above our poor power to add or detract. The world will little note, nor long remember what we say here, but it can never forget what they did here. It is for us the living, rather, to be dedicated here to the unfinished work which they who fought here have thus far so nobly advanced. It is rather for us to be here dedicated to the great task remaining before us—that from these honored dead we take increased devotion to that cause for which they gave the last full measure of devotion—that we here highly resolve that these dead shall not have died in vain—that this nation, under God, shall have a new birth

*of freedom—and that government of the
people, by the people, for the people, shall
not perish from the earth.*

Mr. Lincoln's final words soared on the waiting air
like a dove sent out over water to find land.

There followed a kind of hush, a hesitation, as
though people weren't sure that the president had actually finished. He had spoken less than two minutes.
Then, there was a smattering of formal applause. A pho-
tographer, who had waited nearby to take the president's
picture, was caught off guard. The speech was over and
he was still trying to set up his camera. There was much
milling about as reporters and well-wishers thronged the
platform.

Abraham had trouble seeing through the mist of tears
in his eyes, and soon lost sight of Mr. Lincoln. "We
might as well go on home now, Charity," he said. "I
'spect it's all over but the shoutin'."

Charity hung her head down low, the way she had
during battle, as though she carried the weight of the
world on her back.

Just then, a tall figure moved away from the crowd
and out toward the small copse of trees where Abraham

stood. Blinking away his tears, Abraham whispered, "Charity, that's Mr. Lincoln. And he's comin' this way." He smoothed his ragged coat with trembling hands.

When he reached Abraham, Mr. Lincoln held out his hand. For a moment, Abraham was amazed. Then, trembling, he held out his own hand to the president of the United States. "Abraham Small," he said. "Freeman."

"I saw you out here away from the crowd," said Mr. Lincoln. "I'd like to visit the battlefield before I have to leave Gettysburg, and I'd consider it a kindness if you'd let me borrow your mule."

Abraham bent his neck back to look up at the president. And when Mr. Lincoln looked down at him, Abraham saw the great sadness in his eyes.

"We'd be proud," he replied. Mr. Lincoln stepped up onto the seat of the wagon. Then, with a slow, steady gait, Charity once again trod the same sad fields she'd walked during the battle.

Abraham could scarcely believe that the president of the United States was sitting right next to him in his wagon. Then Mr. Lincoln said, "I'd like to know what you thought about the speech."

Abraham swallowed past the lump in his throat. "It was mighty fine," he said finally.

Mr. Lincoln nodded. "I'm pleased to hear it," he said.

Then Mr. Lincoln asked politely how Abraham came to be there. And Abraham somehow found the courage to actually talk to the president, to tell him about how he drove an ambulance during the battle there. He explained how Charity had carried the wounded from the battleground, and how brave and faithful she'd been. How she'd found the injured and had brought them back for healing. The president listened intently. Then Abraham told him about Lamar and how he'd come to meet him. And how he and Charity had come to save him. "I know I'm 'sposed to hate him. But even if I hated what he stood for, I couldn't hate Lamar. Somehow, I just couldn't view him as my enemy."

Mr. Lincoln gazed around the sere, brown earth. Then he put his big, bony hand on Abraham's arm. "There should be no enemies in this place," he said, quoting a wounded soldier he'd spoken with in a Confederate hospital after the battle at Antietam.

A moment later they reached their destination. "Whoa," said Abraham softly. Charity stopped.

Mr. Lincoln took off his gloves and put them into his hat, which he left on the seat. "I won't be long," he said, climbing down. "I need to pay my respects."

He walked slowly across the field. His tall, gaunt figure stood out in that place, where the trees made no shadows and the earth was torn from battle.

Suddenly, the president dropped to the earth. The whole length of Abraham Lincoln lay stretched out on the cold ground. His great hooded eyelids shut out the pale November sky. He took a deep, shuddering breath.

Charity went over to him. She'd searched out the wounded many times. She nuzzled his neck, looking for warm breath.

Mr. Lincoln opened his eyes and said, "Not to fear, old girl, I'm not hurt. Only my heart is wounded."

Then he rose, brushed the dead grass from his suit, and climbed back up into the wagon.

They rode on for a while in silence. An icy wind blew across the fields. Looking at Charity, Abraham decided that the next money he got his hands on, he'd buy her a thicker blanket for the winter.

"It's getting colder," said the president, putting on his gloves. "Don't you have a hat?"

Abraham replied, "Nossir, not at this time, I don't."

"Here," said Mr. Lincoln, "take mine."

Abraham accepted the gift graciously. He placed the hat on his head and turned to the president.

"Very fine," said Mr. Lincoln.

At the entrance to the cemetery, a throng of people waited. No one was quite sure where the president was, but they weren't expecting to see him in a mule-drawn wagon, so that he was upon them before they realized it. A light cry came from a corner where a group of women and children waited together.

"Charity!" cried Ladysmith, squeezing past the ladies' black hoop skirts. She'd missed the president the night before. She didn't intend to miss him again. "Stop! Wait for me!"

And Charity did, waiting as the small girl in the lilac dress made her way through the crowd and over to the wagon. Abraham lifted her up onto the seat and the president turned to her.

"Mr. President," she said, offering him her bouquet. "I brought you rosebuds."

"You're a precious rosebud yourself," he said, hugging her. A moment later he handed her back down to her mother, who stood at the crowd's edge.

It was nearly dusk when they reached town. The Wills's house was bright with candlelight. Out front, a number of admirers had gathered to bid the president farewell. The same group of men who had made fun of

Abraham and Charity earlier were also there, waiting to escort the president to the train station. Mr. Lincoln stepped down from the wagon and after bidding Abraham farewell, patted Charity on the head. "You're a fine mule," he said. "A mighty fine mule."

Then he was swallowed up in the crowd. Abraham watched as the men on horseback maneuvered for places near the president's carriage. As he passed them on his way home, Abraham smiled and tipped his new hat to them.

"Looks like the bottom rail's on the top, now," he said politely.